P9-CCI-247

BLACKBERRY BUSH

THE WEEPING WILLOW TREE

PICNIC HILL

OL' SNORT

THE PASTURE

THE POND (BABY FROG'S PAD)

THE BABIES' BARN

THE TREE HOUSE

HEN HOUSE

to
Gladys and Edward,
Eva and Sylvester,
who encouraged a young artist
and
Rachel and George,
Elizabeth and Henry,
who established the farms that
inspired this series

Copyright ©1989 by Nate and Susan Butler
Created by Nate Butler
The following names, figure designs, and characters are trademarks of Nate Butler:
Barnyard Babies, Pig-A-Boo, Embraceable Ewe, Cozy Colt, Squeeza-Bull,
Pup-ular Pal, Just Duckie

® —Honey Bear Books is a trademark owned by Honey Bear Productions
Inc., and is registered in the U.S. Patent and Trademark office.

All rights reserved.

Printed in Singapore.

LOOK AND LISTEN

Written by Susan Butler
Illustrated by Nate Butler

MODERN PUBLISHING
A Division of Unisystems, Inc.
New York, New York 10022

COCK-A-DOODLE-DOO
Good morning to you.
It's time to wake up;
There's so much to do!

It's **Mister Rooster** crowing,
Waking up the farm.
Early every morning,
He's the Barnyard Babies' alarm.

SPLISH   SPLASH   SPLISH   SPLASH
What's that noise about?
Still a little sleepy,
The Babies toddle out.

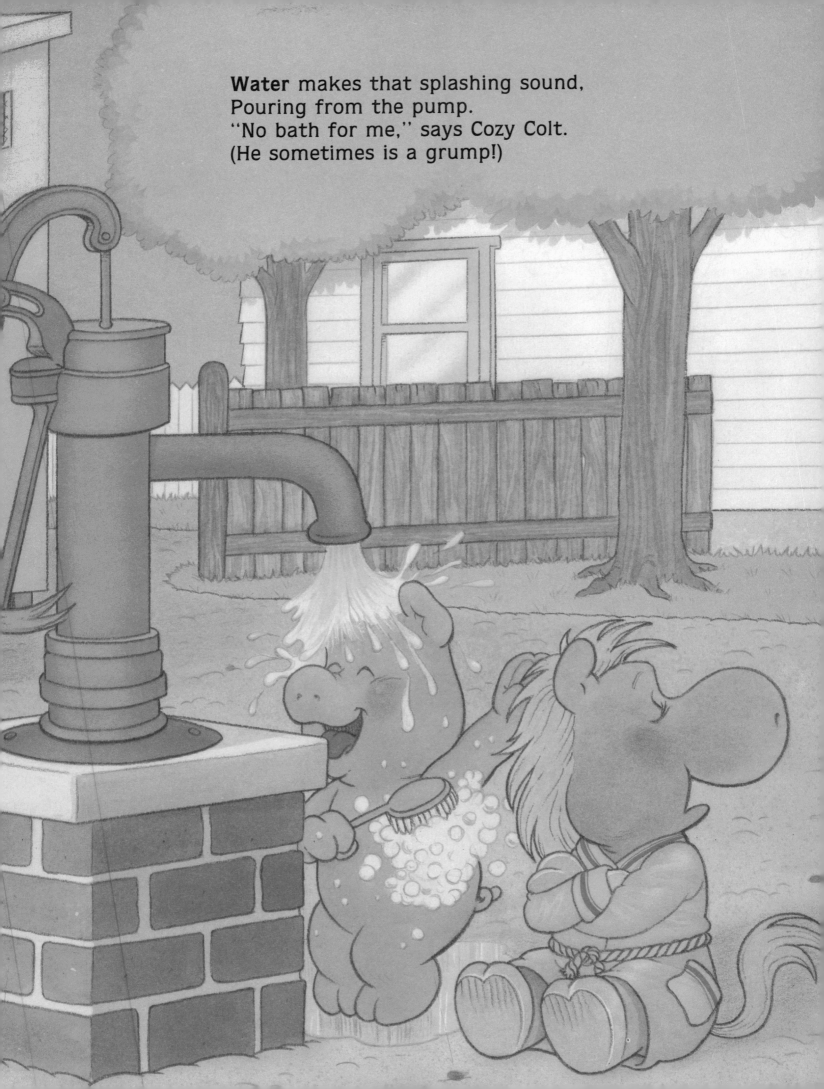

Water makes that splashing sound,
Pouring from the pump.
"No bath for me," says Cozy Colt.
(He sometimes is a grump!)

CLANG   CLANG   CLANG
The Babies know that sound.
"Hurry," says Embraceable Ewe;
They scurry all around.

The **breakfast bell** is ringing.
That means it's time to eat.
Pig-A-Boo gobbles her food;
She isn't very neat!

CHUG CHUG CHUG
What could that sound be?
It's coming from the field!
Squeeza-Bull says: "Follow me!"

Farmer Edwards is on a **tractor**,
Pulling a big plow.
He waves to all the Babies;
Just Duckie takes a bow.

CLUCK   CLUCK   CLUCK
What a lot of chatter!
Pup-ular Pal says, "Let's go see
Who's making such a clatter."

In the yellow hen house,
On their bed of hay,
Chickens sitting in a row,
Laying eggs all day.

BUZZ   BUZZ   BUZZ
Something small flies by.
"Who made that buzzing noise?" asks Ewe.
She looks into the sky.

A **bumblebee** is flying
Around Just Duckie's head.
The bumblebee is heading for
Farmer Edwards' flower bed.

SQUEAK   SQUEAK   SQUEAK
Something just went past.
"Who was that?" asks Cozy Colt.
"He ran by so fast!"

Pup-ular Pal sniffs the trail
And meets a tiny **mouse**,
Who hurries off into the barn
To hide in his small house.

The Barnyard Babies gather
Underneath an apple tree.
"My!" says Pig, "Our farm has
So many things to hear and see!"

COVERED BRIDGE

THE
GOOSEBERRY
BUSH

MISTER
SCARECROW

THE BIG BARN

PIG-A-BOO'S
GARDEN

FARMER
EDWARDS'
HOUSE